Cambridge Lotos Club

A Wreath of Songs

Cambridge Lotos Club

A Wreath of Songs

ISBN/EAN: 9783744774123

Printed in Europe, USA, Canada, Australia, Japan

Cover: Foto ©Andreas Hilbeck / pixelio.de

More available books at **www.hansebooks.com**

A

WREATH OF SONGS

BY THE

CAMBRIDGE LOTOS CLUB.

Cambridge:

DEIGHTON, BELL AND CO.

LONDON: GEORGE BELL AND SONS.

1880

Cambridge:

PRINTED BY C. J. CLAY, M.A.
AT THE UNIVERSITY PRESS.

DEDICATED

TO

OSCAR BROWNING, ESQ.

SENIOR FELLOW OF KING'S COLLEGE,
CAMBRIDGE.

The following pages are composed entirely by a little gathering of Undergraduates. It is hoped therefore that allowance will be made if they be found, according to the old adage, '*non re quam spe laudanda.*'

EDITOR.

PRELUDE.

N dusky eve, cold was the air and still;
Anon the eve-blast smote across the plains
And passed sad-sighing: o'er the waterfloods
The dying day glanced gloriously and died.
Then faded all the glow and flush: and swift
Dense-shadowing gloom o'ercrept the homes of men.

But we, together, passed to distant climes,
The purple mountains of eternal summer,
Lying afar i' the mighty realm of thought;
Where o'er bright lakes pure redolent-breathing winds
Filtered in cooling groves came stealing by;
And golden sundown dyed the sleeping waters,
And tinged the foaming falls with myriad dyes,

Yet sank not into rest: above, the pines,

Cloud-like, on hill-top swayed and swaying slept.

And never breath amid the lotos beds

Sobbed its own requiem to the rustling reeds;

But living lustre o'er the emerald vales

Flashed in the diamond dews and never died—

And inexpressible glory crowned the air,

And dreamy languor drew the inmost being

Into the slumbrous peace of blissful rest.

Then rose calm visions decked in gorgeous tints,

Sapphire and gold and amethystine lights:

And silver-sighing melodies of song,

And trilling of the birds and thrilling cries

Out of the fathomless blue, the dwelling place

Of wandering sprays of cloud and wings of song:

These and the wondrous sight of trailing flights

Of paradisal plumage, slowly sailing

Athwart the restful springs of many lakes,

And mirrored in the immotionate calm beneath.

While sweeter far than cloud-sung carollings
Bright heralds of the radiant hours of prime,
And lowlier than the plaintive voice of eve,
Out of the moss-dells of the fairy groves
Came soul-like utterances entrancing soft,
Came silver-sighing harmonies entwined
In varied note perfection absolute.

     *   *   *   *   *   *

Wherefore, arising when earth's morn returned,
Dazed in the maze of many-tinted glows
From crimson bloom and snow-crowned lily flowers
O'er fleet-winged waters waving ceaselessly,
And sleep-rocked tarns and myriad forms of beauty—
Visions of yester eve returning robed,
Robed in still glories of the dreamland dales—
We—gathering from the relics of those dreams
That lay about the halls of memory—
Have woven this our varied wreath of song,
Soft dedication to the dreams of air:

And unto whatsoever mind may sound

In harmony with ours—we dedicate

Ere it be faded, as perchance it may

Fade, fall and mix i' the trodden dust of man,

We dedicate, and proffer unto hands

That shall receive it for the sake of song,

And treasure it as promise of the years,

And praise the flowers in hope that aftertides

Shall view the full-bloomed autumn gathering,

When   fruit,   we   trust,   shall   take   the   place   of

    flowers—

To these alone we dedicate with joy

This love-toil of sweet hours—this wreath of song.

THE LYRIC OF THE REED.

I SAT by a river bank, when the woods were vocal
　　and sweet;
With the hawthorns above my head, and forget-me-
　　nots at my feet.

When the warm west wind just stirred the flag-
　　flowers about the brink,
And the twilight's crimson rim o'er the hills began
　　to sink.

When the flush of the day was low, and the Star
　　of Love first gleamed,
Like a firefly over the vale, and the crescent moon-
　　rays streamed.

Then I took from the sandy marge a reed where
the rushes grew,
Palm-like above the river, golden and green in
hue :

And I fashioned it into form, and I played on it
like a Pan,
And its whispers began to mingle with the depths
of my inner man.

And there in the twilight hour, when the odorous
winds blew faint,
I seemed to gather this meaning, from its soft and
thrilling plaint—

"The Poet is Nature's child, he lives in a world
alone,
And the eager crowd rush on, nor list to his mystic
tone :

"And the sons of the Iron Age laugh at his deepest
    song,
But he stands apart from the mob, from the shallow-
    hearted throng,

"Who scorn what in happier days in the past
    enchanted years,
Would have gladdened the souls of the Great, and
    melted them into tears.

"We have fallen on sordid times, when the Earth
    is all common-place,
When to sing is a shameful waste, and to link into
    subtle grace

"The pent-up passions and powers of the inmost
    soul is neglect,
For this is an Age of bronze, and lacquer, and
    clique, and sect!

"When Virtue is second rate, and Love but a
    brain-sick dream,
When Lucre runs riot, and Vice engulfs the world
    in its stream.

"O Dante and Petrarch, methinks, from the weird
    song-land could ye glance
O'er this money-stricken earth, that heeds not Song
    or Romance ;

"That scoffs at poetic lays and tramples them in
    the dust,
Ye would weep great drops of blood o'er this æon
    of Gold and Lust.

"O Shakespeare and Milton ! ye too have felt the
    distrustful age,
Ye too have languished in pain o'er the tear-blotted
    story page.

"Yet heed not, oh aching heart, though thy spirit
repines and grieves,
The blackest cloud looms ere dawn, and Hope in
the deep East weaves

"The dream of a golden morn, that over the world
will burst,
When the nations will hang on the breaths of the
Poets, as in the erst:

"When the sons of culture will walk in the gardens
of Poesy,
'Neath the spell of the old-world's trust, in the
unborn years yet to be."

    *   *   *   *   *   *   *   *

The soul-stirring music ceased, the moon rose over
the vale,
And all was still save the thrill of the warbling
nightingale;

But there by the river brink, with the sleeping
    flowers on the slope,
The lay of the reed returned, and whispered—
    "Courage and Hope."

                          a.

A MEMORY.

NOT in the summer days
  When the noontide blazes
Through a filmy haze,
  On the poor parched daisies,
  And the glaring ways—

When you tire of play,
  Tire of talk and laughter,
Of the languid day
  And what may be after,
  All but sleep, you say—

When the years to be
　　Shadow not your pleasure
In the world you see
　　Full of laughing leisure—
　　Think not then of me.

Not in dancing time,
　　Or in time of singing
Full of sound and rhyme,
　　And the thrill of singing
　　Strings and feet that chime—

But when coming day
　　Brings an end of dances,
Beauty fades away,
　　Lamps and flowers and fancies,
　　As the world grows grey—

When the sound of wheels
Wearies you in going,
And the landscape feels
Strange beyond all knowing,
As the dawning steals—

When the last stars shine
Faint as dying embers,
May my soul divine
That your heart remembers
Any word of mine?

As the grey clouds grow
Into gold above you,
Will your dreaming know
What I feel that love you,
I that love you so?

b.

DULL DAYS.

SOME days are dull, the sky nor smiles nor weeps,
 'Twill only frown;
Sullen suspense her weary watches keeps
 Till night comes down.

Some days of life are very dull and dreary,
 Nor sad nor bright;
The heart remains monotonously weary
 Until the night.

Then comes the night of nature, and of sorrow,
 And a dark fight;
The world sees not the struggle, and the morrow
 Is often bright.

C.

S.

A POLITICAL ALLEGORY.

ONCE there was a famous nation
    With a long and glorious past:
Very splendid was its station,
    And its territory vast.
It had gained the approbation,
The applause and admiration
Of the states who'd had occasion
In a time of tribulation
And of disorganisation
    To observe it standing fast
Without any trepidation,
    Firm and faithful to the last.

Came a time of dire distraction,
    Full of terror and despair,
When a delicate transaction
    Called for unexampled care;

And the people were directed,

Both the well and ill affected,

To a wholly unexpected

And surprising course of action

    Based on motives new and rare

(Being governed by a faction,

    As they generally were).

In a little time the nation

    Had a chance of saying whether

It and its administration

    Seemed inclined to pull together;

And it spoke its mind with vigour :—

    "Such disgraceful conduct must

Everlastingly disfigure

    Future annals, and disgust

Evermore the candid student:

You have been unwise, imprudent,

    Pusillanimous, unjust,

And neglectful of the glory,
   Appertaining to our name
Till this melancholy story
   Put a period to our fame."

So this faction, disappointed,
   Lost the national good graces,
And their rivals were anointed
   And were set in the high places.
Pretty soon arose conditions
   Most embarrassing and hard,
And the party politicians
   Had to be upon their guard.
Illegitimate ambitions,
Democratic rhetoricians,
Persons prone to base submissions,
Men of warlike dispositions,
   And a host of wary foes

Compassed round the ruling faction :
But a certain line of action
    They incontinently chose :
And with great determination
Wrought it out with acclamation,
Till the national taxation
    Not unnaturally rose.

To the nation soon occurred an
    Opportunity of saying
What they thought about the burden
    Which the government was laying
On their shoulders ; and they said it
    In uncompromising terms :—
"Your behaviour would discredit
    Tigers, crocodiles, or worms.
You have ruined and disgraced us,
And successfully effaced us
From the proud commanding station,

Where the zeal and penetration
  Of our ancestors had placed us.
Go! we are a ruined nation,
But, before our dissolution
We pronounce your condemnation—
Sappers of our constitution,
Slayers of our reputation!"

But the nation—mark the moral,
  For its value is untold—
During each successive quarrel
  Grew and prospered as of old.

d.

AFTERNOON CHAPEL.

CLOUD overhead and darkening of the skies,
    Yet the glow lingers on the pictured panes
    Reluctantly, and gold and ruby wanes
From robes of saints and royal blazonries,
But let the monotones of prayer arise,
    And the choir's music, louder than the rain's,
    Blend with the organ. Though the wind com-
        plains,
Without the windows still its wailing dies.
Yet must we leave at length the goodly fane,
    And as the closing of the carven door
    Shuts in the vision of the shrine dim-lit,
We meet the passionate weeping of the rain;
    The wind's old wail is sadder than before,
    And nothing in the music answers it.

b.

LES JARDINS DES TUILERIES.

FAR away I close my eyes,
  At the dying hour of day,
See again thy moon-lit skies—
                    Jardin des Tuileries.

Roam beneath thy orange-bowers,
  See thy silvern fountains play,
Foaming by the dew-dimm'd flowers—
                    Jardin des Tuileries.

Wander on thy broad white walks,
  When the earth is filled with May;
Linger in discursive talks—
                    Jardin des Tuileries.

Hand in hand again we steal,
    By thy violet-scented way,
When the bells for vespers peal—
               Jardin des Tuileries.

Wheresoe'er my home may be,
    Whatsoe'er the world may say,
Thou wilt crown my phantasy—
               Jardin des Tuileries.

                      a.

NUPTA.

DELIGHTFUL days of converse sweet
    When more than sister, back returned
    She soothed the hearts that long had yearned
Her voice, her look, her smile to greet!

With love's rich lesson in her eyes,
    And on her lips his language rare,
    She came, a breath of purer air,
A star from some serener skies.

No longer child, but woman grown,
  With warmer heart, if that could be,
  Instinct with larger sympathy,
Her spring-tide graces wider blown.

She came and went : we chafed no more,
  With her great gladness satisfied,
  And set again the window wide
That our white dove might landward soar !

                  f.

THE WHEEL OF LIFE.

Oh, yes ! Life is a weary wheel,
  That turns for ever in the stream ;
Sometimes the currents rage and reel,
  And glide sometimes with silvery gleam.

But unlike every other wheel,

   E'en those that ne'er in rest remain,

Life spins its never tiring reel;

   But no part e'er comes round again.

                         c.

THE TOWN BRIDGE.

STILL, so still:

   Where the grey dim arches start

   Nothing beats except my heart;

   Down beneath the waters part

Silently, silently.

Still, so still:

   On the mist-robed calm below

   Sways the eve-light to and fro,

   And the bright stars come and go

Silently, silently.

Still, so still :

    Rest beneath their bosom lies,

    Sleep of sleep for brimming eyes ;

    One deep plunge, and sorrow flies

Silently, silently !

Still, so still :

    From the waters turn and gaze

    O'er true eve-lights thro' the haze,

    Where stars move eternal ways ·

Silently, silently,—

Still, so still :

    Come away, and let us go ;

    Surely there is rest below,

    Where the slumberer sleeps from woe

Silently, silently.

e.

MIDNIGHT.

A SPACE of blue unfathomable night,
   Solemn with sense of all the stars unseen·—
   Veiled shades of banks, and shadow-bridge between,
And mist-encircled blurs and points of light—
The river rolling in mysterious might,
   And dim as dreams that doubt of what they mean,
   And boats and men, as ghosts of what has been :
All this we feel, with deeper sense than sight.
Day would give back dull roofs and blackened
     towers ;
   A sullen stream, grey lightless piles of stone ;
   And fierce pursuit of pleasures, nought enjoyed.
Better the mystic moonless midnight hours,
   And the dim vision, limitless and lone,
   Of the vast city asleep, and vaster void.

                            b.

THE GLEANER'S CONSOLATION.

As I was looking on the golden harvest
  And on the gleaners gathering the grain,
I thought how trifling was the gleaners' portion
  Beside the reapers' heavy, creaking wain.
But turning homeward, dreamily reflecting,
  I said "The gleaners share, tho' it be less,
Is none the less of the same precious substance
  As those before have reaped in rich excess."
And with this came a thought that half rebuked me,
  And yet encouraged, saying "In this age
There is a harvest of rich thoughts for reaping:
  The reapers are the poet, seer, and sage."
"I cannot be a reaper; I must follow,
  And glean some ears of the immortal grain:
Walk where the great have walked before, and stooping,
  With patience seek the fragments that remain."

                                        C.

GOOD FRIDAY, 1880.

O MAN of men, O world-dividing Name,
O bruisèd Body, fevered with the shame,
There, 'twixt the earth and heavens, yet crowned
    with fame,
    Haggard and pale, I see Thee crucified.

I mark that blood-fringed brow, that wreath of
    thorns,
That far-off look, while mockers shout their scorns;
Perchance Thou dreamest of the vanished morns
    Of youth, when life was budding in its pride.

O sacred Face, O gracious Nazarene,
Man-like in death, yet God-like in Thy mien,
Around Thy Head a Light of mystic sheen
    Shines through the ages, glorifying Space.

And I would carry, in my inmost core,

A reflex from its glow, to mellow more,

The Flame that never glowed on sea or shore!

Yet sanctifies, unseen, the desert place.

a.

"THE NIGHT IS AS CLEAR AS THE DAY."

THE night is as clear as the day:

O golden the fair clime must be

Where never a shadow of bitterness lay

In the land of the buoyant and free!

Henceforth when the glooms of despair,

Dense-shadowing, over me stray,

I'll sing for the peace of the paradise there,

Where the night is as clear as the day!

e.

PREJUDICE.

THE faults of others as they pass,
  Are with much profit known,
When, in reflection's faithful glass,
  We view them as our own.

But Prejudice ah ! who shall find,
  By this self-searching plan?
We note another's darkened mind,
  Our own we never can.

For in our reason's searching light
  Their blindness stands exposed;
But who with any mortal sight,
  Can see—his own eyes closed?

c.

NOCTURNE.

THE twilight ebbs across the fading sky,
And the tide sinks and the long beach is dry,
  Save where the bitter pools and streamlets steep
The barren sand, like tears of misery
That the sad sea is weeping, even as I
  For pain of love and sorrow without sleep.

I lean into the night with panting lips;
There is no air to shake the sails of ships
  And rouse the beating pulses of the deep;
Only a sound of the thin brook that drips,
And sighing ripples on the sandy strips,
  Moved by the moving tide that knows not sleep.

Yet now the sea is still and pacified,
The sighing softens as the sands grow wide,
  At the far end of the long backward sweep;

The utter ebb and pausing of the tide;

For the sea-winds and all the waves have died,

   And the world's trouble almost seems to sleep.

Last night I dreamed that I lay happily

Where the deep water and the foam are free,

   And all strange lovely creatures swim and creep;

My hair was as the sea-weed in the sea,

And the green light was tender over me,

   So I was glad to feel myself asleep.

It may be thus that I shall seek for rest

When the full tide comes calling from the west,

   With sound of voices not as those that weep;

It may be this shall soothe the heaving breast,

The lips unloved and the hot hands unpressed,

   For surely in the ocean there is sleep.

And yet, O eyes forgetful of your faith!
O love, will you remember but in death?

   Is there no echo that your heart can keep?
The tide has turned; and with the tide its breath
Comes landward whispering to me and saith,

   Love is not lost that only seems to sleep.

                        b.

TO DISAPPOINTMENT.

OH Disappointment, how unkind,
   How foolish also to upbraid thee;
For Love, who now has long been blind,
   Before his eyes were dazzled, made thee.

And now thou art of all his train
   The wisest and the kindest creature;
And must, despite thy name, remain
   His one undisappointing feature.

By pleasure's lips we'd fain be kissed,
  And failing will not then caress thee;
But seeing, after, what we've missed,
  How thankfully we turn and bless thee!

c.

WRITTEN BY THE GRAVE OF GEORGE HEATH, THE MOORLAND POET IN HORTON CHURCHYARD.

HERE 'neath the low-lying heap,
  With the musical May all around,
Stretched in a slumberless sleep,
  Wrapped in the dark moorland ground,
  When the earth with the wind-flowers is crown'd,
He rests where the violets peep.

One, whom the world never knew,
  Whose chords scarcely rippled the breeze;

One of the song-gifted few,
  Lying here 'neath the dim aspen trees,
  Dead! while the chant of the bees
And the wild birds steal over the dew.

In the days that have summer'd and flower'd,
  In the years when his youth felt the stream
Of the pent-up passions, and dower'd
  His soul with the poet's dream,
  And the stars shed a mystical gleam,
And all Nature with love was empower'd;

Did his arduous mind pant and yearn
  As he paced by the moon-shadowed ways;
Did his mellowing Muse ever burn,
  As she whispered his handful of lays,
  For the meed of the popular praise,
And the glorified funeral urn?

I know not—his life was a thread
   In the woof Culture weaves hour by hour;
The cowslips droop over his head,
   And the sun-flush broods o'er the church tower,
   And Spring fills the earth with its power,
But the singer lies here 'mid the dead!

a.

'Ηδέως ἀνέχεσθε τῶν ἀφρόνων.

GLADLY, gladly ye suffer fools,
   Seeing that ye yourselves are wise!
Looking down the throng as they struggle along,
Misled by their foolish faith in the wrong—
   Oh! verily ye are wise!

Immotionate shrines of the balanced mind,
From your cold heights ye gaze down,
With a chilling sneer, on the holy fear
That sheds to the nightstar many a tear,—
Or at best with a scathing frown.—

Oh blind, thrice blind, when the heart is strung,
Ye know no more than I:
Then veil your scorn ere the day be born
And ye yourselves, with plight forlorn,
Are dazed at the flaming sky!—

Am I bitter?—Ah! well, but ye cut the heart
With the cold keen blade of scorn;
Ye search for light—till the days be bright—
God knows it is dark enough in the night—
Peace then—for the day shall dawn!

c.

GREATNESS.

THEIR names are great and shall endure,
  Whose lives are crowned with noble thought;
But they, tho' crownless and obscure,
  Are greater who have nobly wrought.

                                        c.

TO E. R. C.

SHOULD you be taken from my side away,
  Beyond my ken and where I may not come,
Rest in the falling shadows of the day,
  Where autumn whirlings are the sad year's sum—

Then—I perchance, all dim of fears and tears,
  Weeping apart, should give to God my moan;
You meantime slumbering where the spirit hears
  The angel clarion and the golden tone.

Then—for an hour, if God would will it so,
  Oh may you leave the sight and light of love;
And o'er the sunflamed snowcloud downward flow
  Spirit to spirit from the Unknown Above.

Then—in the flush and hushing of the eve,
  Dreamlike, thy radiant soul, at one with mine,
Should breathe the unseen glorious things that weave
  In faith's deep vision fashion most divine.

Then I should hear which way the spirit fled
  When closed thine eyes and life's sweet lamp
    burned low,
When some unknown but awful thing of dread
  Moved in the eve and bade the spirit go.

Then should I hear what passing thought of me,
  What lingering joy of earth's departed hours,
Soft nestling rested in the being free
  E'en when ascending toward the flaming towers.

Come then, if thou shouldst die, if so may be—
A kindly hand to guide athro' the gloom,
Else, leave a little slumber space for me
Side by thy side within the mossy tomb.

e.

FLOTSAM.

THE sands that bury and forget,
The sea's forgetfulness of foam,
The sky that knew us never yet,
Stand round about our homeless home.
Wet weeds upon unnoted graves,
Heavens clenched in clouds of pitiless grey,
And refluent ruin of white waves,—
These are the words they say.

Earth can but say the speech of years,
Slow days and years and times that tire
With trouble of man's fruitless tears
And unattainable desire ;

And each man answers back the earth

    With life whose limits have but held

One only gain of little worth,

    A kiss unchronicled.

b.

OVER THE BEAUTIFUL WATERS.

"The world is void of thee but Space
Is something holier than before."

OVER the beautiful waters my love has wandered
    away,

Where the foam lines brighten and lighten in glow
    of the day,

Where the plains of the waters around and about
    him lay,

No land on the dim horizon, no isle where the
    billows play.

And I shall weep him and weep him, because I
know that he lies

With his fair head on the deep weeds, and the
films of death in his eyes;

I shall weep him, while o'ersweeps him every
tempest, as it flies,

And the sullen storm bemoaning, on his wave-tost
resting dies.

Over the beautiful waters, afar on the glittering
plain

Merrily dashes the sunbeam, and lightly plashes the
rain,

But below them and beneath them, where the
pearl shells remain.

Lies my love and sleeps my love, and I shall not
know him again.

e.

AU CHATEAU DE SANG.

"La voyez-vous croître
La tour du vieux cloître,
Et le grand mur noir
Du royal manoir?"

ALFRED DE VIGNY.

A LEAGUE from Tours, o'er the moon-shadow'd hill,
 Thy gloomy pile frowns on the wooded steep;
Thy gardens with sweet scents the still air fill,
 Beneath there rolls the river dark and deep.

Thy tinkling fountains murmur lullabies,
 Through one eternal summer-sabbath eve;
In thy dim cloister-walks the low light dies,
 And wandering in the enchanted gloom, I weave,

In measured rhymes, the story of the Past—
 What wondrous deeds of prowess hast thou seen!
Here where a glory from the moon is cast,
 Here where the rose-leaves flutter on the green,

How many a tournament, and feat of power

    Has thrown a lustre, and a spark of fame;

And, from the oriel-niche of that grey tower,

    How many a white hand waved a glad acclaim !

And in your marble chapel, rich in gold

    And silver banners, many a nameless saint

Has knelt, when star-beams flickered o'er the wold,

    And chaunted, till the dawn, his lowly plaint !

Forgotten visions of the Erst return;

    The dreamy legends of the ancient days

Crowd on my fancy, in my memory burn,

    Mingle their voices with my random lays.

Yet thou, through cloud and spring-bloom, still
      loom'st o'er,

    The shining valley and the vine-clad steep,

Thy babbling streams may gleam with purple gore

    Thy glen may echo cannon's booming deep.

Thy forest mazes hid the fleeing foe,
  Thy groves be desecrate by spoilers' feet;
But thou remainest, 'neath the red sun's glow,
  Strong in thy beauty through the storm and sleet.

Beside thy antique dial, hand-in-hand
  With him—the latest of thy lordly race—
When Tours and Loches are wrapped in sleep, I
      stand,
  And gaze upon thy stately art and grace.

Through the sweet night, we roam about thy walks,
  While the caressing air blows faint and cold,
Pacing a while, in meditative talks,
  And dreaming of the knightly deeds of old.

Le château de sang,
    Tours.

                                        a.

DISSATISFACTION.

I.

WHEN life is young, and might be happy,
  The brightest joys we're wont to miss,
While idly painting, from our fancy,
  The picture of some future bliss.

II.

In after years, when joys are scarcer,
  And with some taste of sorrow tainted,
We lose the most in useless sighing
  O'er pictures only fancy painted.

C.

PUELLULÆ.

The rose flashed out in a world of flowers,
   With sweet lips cleft to smile:
And to her the South spake low in showers
   Of a love that knew no guile.

But the pale snow-bloom, she dwelt alone,
   And ever scanned the sky,
A frozen queen on her mountain-throne,
   With a meek mysterious eye.

And which was the fairer?—well-a-day!—
   And which made more delight?
For red and rare was the rose, men say,
   But the snow-bloom rare and white.

f.

DESPAIR.

HER eyes were hollow with a depth of pain,
   Her face was pallid as her pinched white lips,
   Her bloodless hands were linked in stony grips ;
She wandered 'lone beside the moaning main.

Her naked feet were bleeding on the stones,
   Her swan-like neck peered o'er the sun-dyed sea ;
   She gazed a while in speechless misery,
Then murmured in unconscious monotones :—

"Ah me, sweet Death ! but, why so long delay ?
   I fain would feel thy icy kiss, and weep
   My frozen sorrow on thy breast, and sleep
In dreamless quiet, through an endless day.

" I fain would lie beneath the daisied mound,
   Hearing, yet heeding not, in that dark bed,
   The foot-falls in the long grass overhead,
Wending their way athwart the holy ground.

"Ah me! alas! the summer-coloured hours
    Are grey and arid, for my soul is sore;
    Ah me! to deaden thought for evermore,
To slumber still beneath the moon-kiss'd flowers.

"I hear no answer from the broad-blown bay,
    No faint response from zones of dying light,
    No music from the voices of the night,
No song of hope from out the first blue ray."

So wept the maiden, with sob-broken staves,
    At length a silence fell—and in the night,
    Beneath the stars I found her cold and white,
Dead, by the rippling of the star-lit waves.

a.

IN THE HAMMOCK.

THERE is a tremor in the windless air

    That scarce may stir the leaves above my head ;

    The weariness of sunlight lies like lead

On the gold-green of grasses ; and the glare

Of scarlet flowers burns all the flower-beds bare,

    Save of that blinding splendour of sheer red ;

    And I methinks am living and not dead,

But other life there seems not anywhere,

Yet somewhere surely are the nightly throngs

    Of those that toil and sorrow and are wise

    More than my thought can ever understand ;

Less seem they than the least of dreamy songs

    In the closed book of songs unread that lies

    Under the hammock fallen from my hand.

b.

THE TWO BARQUES.

A BARQUE roll'd on across the sea,
    Deep-veiled in storm and rain;
For the steersman let the helm go free
    As tho' all hope were vain.

The white-crown'd billows foamed and tossed
    And fled the barque alone:
Then vanished, hopeless, helpless, lost,
    Far in the deep unknown.

*   *   *

Another barque the waters passed
    The storm beat stern and strong
But the steersman held the rudder fast
    And sped the deep along.

Then broke the gloom, the sun arose
  Fell wind and rested strand ;
The harbour'd barque had found repose
  And the steersman gained the land.

*   *   *.

I hold it nobler far to keep
  And clutch the helm and wait for day—
Than when the first fierce tempests sweep
  Fling hope and trust and faith away.

e.

MY WISH.

(Written in an Album.)

WHAT good now, never wished before,
Wish I for thee were held in store?
For virtue, beauty, wit and health,
To have the coarse desire for wealth,
Have all been wished full many a time

In every mood and tune of rhyme;
And I would like to wish for you
Something that is both sweet and new :
But 'tis so hard to be concise
And shape into some neat device
My wishes, that would crowd a book,
To suit an album's modest nook.
My mind with doubts so sorely fraught,
In haste I'd better wish thee naught;
I doubt—'tis this that makes me falter,—
There's aught that I could wisely alter :
Then shall I wish thee aught? not I.
Some greater mind will doubtless try;
But I feel far too much afraid
To spoil a life divinely made.
But this I wish, I fear too much,
Unvaried by the slightest touch,
The only wish that seems to strike me,
I wish, in truth, that more were like thee.

C.

TO —.

THAT was a golden day when first thy hand
Clasped mine in one long pressure, though the
leaves
Of autumn strewed the dark blue misty land,
And though the fields were bare, and drooping
sheaves
Of corn were housed beneath the frosted eaves:
Yet that bright hour shines still; my heart un-
weaves,
Grows vocal into song, as though a wand
Of magic minstrel touched its iron greaves,
And I recall to its enchanted end,
That joyous morn, when first you called me Friend.

What bliss was mine! I trod on silver feet,
I close my eyes at eve and image thee,
Seated again, in yonder sloping seat,
Conversing of the dreams of Liberty:

Dear Friend—but all that thou hast been to me,

Thou canst not know ; yet, worthless though it be,

I consecrate this lyric, little meet

To claim thy thoughts, but when Philosophy

May pall and weary, let these idle rhymes,

Rewake the memories of forgotten times.

a.

THE THISTLE.

MARK you the thistle-seeds, borne on the air

Hither and thither and heaven knows where ;

Thro' the still woodlands slowly they stray

O'er field and river floating away.

Surely next summer-time, white in the sun,

Thousands shall flourish where now you see one :

You cannot number them floating away,

Think you to count them a year from to-day ?

Look in your heart, friend, there you will find,
Seeds of much evil afloat on the mind.
Crush every root of them—cast them away!
Think you to count them a year from to-day?

May be another year, you'll look again,
Trying to root them out, struggling in vain,
What if you find that it can't be undone?
Find many flourish where now there is one?

This is the hour then, for harvest is near,
See how they sail in the fall of the year!
Root them out, cast them out, fling them away,
Never a weed be found next summer day!

e.

A BALLAD OF A GARDEN.

WITH flash of the light oars swiftly plying
　　The sharp prow furrows the watery way,
The ripples reach to the bank in dying,
　　And soft shades shudder and long lights play,
　　In the still dead heat of the drowsy day,
As on I sweep with the stream that flows
　　By languid lilies and boats astray
To the garden of grace whose name none knows.

There ever a whispering wind goes sighing
　　Filled with scent of the new-mown hay
Over the flower-hedge peering and prying,
　　Wooing the rose as with words that pray;
　　And the waves from the broad white river bay
Slide through clear channels to dream and doze,
　　Or rise in a fountain's silver spray
In the garden of grace whose name none knows.

The sweet white rose with the red rose vying
   Blooms when the summer follows the May,
Till the stream be hid by the lost leaves lying,
   That autumn shakes where the lilies lay.
   But now all bowers and beds are gay,
And no rain ruffles the flower that blows,
   And still on the water soft streams stay
In the garden of grace whose name none knows.

L'envoi.

Before the blue of the sky grows grey
   And the frayed leaves fall from the faded rose,
Love's lips shall sing what the day-dreams say
   In the garden of grace whose name none knows.

b.

HOME.

Home! so he cried and swift the bounding keel
Drove thro' the dark, and cut the chilling foam,
 And dashed it o'er his brow,
 But he—soft murmured Home!

His fair locks fluttered in the frenzied gale,
Like thunder fell the billows into foam,
 But on the crested wave
 He rode—soft sighing Home!

A long rift grew across the leaden night,
And tipped with silver ray the rising foam,
 Then thro' the rift he sped
 And passed—soft echoing Home!

* * *

Then, in the morning gladness, I arose.

There was a pale face, paler than the foam,

    But I wept not that morn :—

    "He had but journeyed Home!"

                         c.

THE wreath is woven, may its fragrance steal,

Sweet as the breath of lilies in the Spring,

From where the far-famed city brinks the Cam,

Eastward and westward, bearing rich perfume

Of buds of Hope and Beauty, and perchance

Wafting its odours down the stream of Song.

CAMBRIDGE: PRINTED BY C. J. CLAY, M.A., AT THE UNIVERSITY PRESS.